A Greek Reader for Chase and Phillips

A Greek Reader for Chase and Phillips

Selections from Antiquity

Brian Schmisek

WIPF & STOCK · Eugene, Oregon

A GREEK READER FOR CHASE AND PHILLIPS
Selections from Antiquity

Wipf & Stock
An Imprint of Wipf and Stock Publishers
199 W. 8th Ave., Suite 3
Eugene, OR 97401

www.wipfandstock.com

PAPERBACK ISBN: 978-1-4982-3850-2
HARDCOVER ISBN: 978-1-4982-3852-6

Manufactured in the U.S.A.

This Greek Reader is dedicated to Carol Andreini and Frank Russell, professors whose love of Classics inspired my own.

Contents

Preface

THE IDEA FOR THIS reader germinated decades ago when I was an undergraduate learning Ancient Greek under the patient tutelage of Dr. Carol Andreini (now at the University of Mary in North Dakota) and with the textbook by Chase and Phillips. At the time, I wished for more practice reading Greek, as Chase and Phillips provides only a few sentences with each lesson. A supplementary reader also seemed to me appropriate for the introductory Latin textbook by Wheelock. By the time I finished my undergraduate degree, I was delighted to see that Anne Groton and James May's *Thirty-Eight Latin Stories*, designed to accompany Wheelock's Latin grammar, had been published. As I taught Latin at various levels, that reader (now in its sixth edition) was a handy tool for the students' acquisition of the ancient language. By the time I was in graduate school at the University of Mississippi I had been exposed to many more primary Latin and Greek textbooks and grammars. But many of the Greek introductory texts lacked an accompanying reader. So I proposed to write a thesis that would bring together a variety of readings for different introductory Greek grammars. My mentor and thesis director, Dr. Frank Russell (now at Transylvania University in Kentucky) was open to the idea. So this present work is derived in part from my M.A. thesis. After completing the thesis I moved on to other projects and scarcely gave it another thought. Only recently, upon meeting the good people at Wipf and Stock, was there momentum to publish a reader focused squarely on accompanying Chase and Phillips. My only regret is the delay of two decades due to my own inattention in bringing this project to fruition. It is hoped that this reader will aid the first year student of Greek who is fortunate to be learning with Chase and Phillips. May that student also have an instructor as patient as Dr. Andreini and as encouraging as Dr. Russell.

Abbreviations

(alphabetical by abbreviation)

acc	accusative
Act.	Active
Adv.	Adverb
Aor.	Aorist
ca.	circa (around)
cf.	see, by way of comparison
d.	died
dat	dative
f	feminine
Fut.	Future
gen	genitive
Impft.	Imperfect
Impv.	Imperative
Inf.	Infinitive
m	masculine
Mid.	Middle
n	neuter
n.	note
nom	nominative
Opt.	Optative
pers.	person
pl.	plural
Pass.	Passive
Perf.	Perfect
Pres.	Present
Ptc.	Participle
sing.	singular

Introduction

THIS READER IS DESIGNED to supplement the Alston H. Chase and Henry Phillips, Jr., *A New Introduction to Greek* (Third Edition Revised and Enlarged; Cambridge, Massachusetts/London, England: Harvard University Press, 1961) by keying short passages from ancient Greek to specific points of grammar presented in the book.

Many modern methods of teaching Greek, and even Latin, almost presuppose by their presentation of grammar that the student learns most effectively not by rote memorization of case endings and rigorous drilling of verb forms, but rather, by translating many lines of "easy" Greek with points of grammar furtively "slipped in."[1] In contrast, throughout the late 19th and early 20th centuries, classicists knew the value of routine and regular review. "Frequent reference to the grammar is the only sure means of fixing in the mind the important principles of syntax."[2] I believe it is only through this exercise of translating "real Greek" that the student will come not only to find a deeper understanding of the differing moods of the verbs, but also the more difficult task of acquiring a feeling for "the finer distinctions of the Greek tenses."[3] Thus, the text unites pedagogical methods at work in some modern textbooks[4] with the wisdom expressed by those classicists who have gone before us.

Modernity requires that we neither merely parrot methods of the past, nor discard them in favor of crossword puzzles and word finds,[5] but rather, incorporate proven methods into our present system of education. So, although I agree with Goodwin and

1. E.g. Ullman, et al., *Latin for Americans*; Balme and Morwood, *Oxford Latin Course*; and Balme and Lawall, *Athenaze*.

2. Goodwin and White, *The First Four Books of Xenophon's Anabasis*, iii.

3. Adams, *Lysias*, 5.

4. E.g., Wheelock, *Wheelock's Latin Grammar*.

5. Balme and Morwood, *Oxford Latin Course*, 11 and 61.

White that "it is highly desirable to use as small a portion as possible of the classic literature as a *corpus vile* for the more minute dissection, and to enable pupils at the earliest possible moment to read Greek and Latin with an appreciative mind,"[6] I do think that we must broaden the *corpus vile* beyond the first four books of Xenophon's *Anabasis*. "Beginners today must early meet Democritus, Plato, Thucydides, and Herodotus if they are ever to be encouraged to go farther."[7] Thus the reader incorporates passages from various authors in order to attract and capture the imagination of the student who may then early on develop a relationship with those giants of Greek antiquity by translating their very words, with minimal help from a side gloss.

Reviewing a grammatical construction in a translation exercise reinforces the rules of grammar covered in the textbook. In my own experience teaching at both the college and high school level, I find that students are often encouraged by reading such passages of extended length with limited, if any, emendations. The translation of sentences in grammar books is often accompanied by the sighs of students grappling with monolinear phrases, struggling in the midst of a nebulous cloud of forms, genders, tenses, constructions, authors, and syntax to make sense of the language. The task of putting together a supplemental Greek text is therefore deemed appropriate, indeed necessary, for the modern student of Greek to have at his or her disposal an important if not essential tool for learning and comprehending the language of ancient Greece in a context of historical and anecdotal pericopes germane to the grammar presented in a particular lesson.

The readings are drawn from Diogenes Laertius, Xenophon, Plato, Plutarch and the *Septuagint*. These have been chosen for many reasons, not only to reinforce grammar but even moreso to inculcate a love of Greek and the stories from that language. To that end, there are several about Socrates, one story about Caesar and his early encounter with pirates, something about Plato from a biographer centuries later, and as a nod to those who learn Greek to

6. Goodwin and White, *The First Four Books of Xenophon's Anabasis*, iv.

7. Chase and Phillips, *A New Introduction to Greek*, v.

translate biblical material, two more famous readings from the *Septuagint*. The fundamental parameters for selection include: the use of Attic Greek (with the exceptions of the *Septuagint* and Diogenes); the contribution of the particular text to a knowledge of Greek history, especially with regard to specific persons and vignettes about them; a fairly simple Greek style subject to minimal modifications; and a good, relevant, interesting story. With the exception of a rather straightforward Psalm (which itself is a translation of Hebrew), poetry has not been used for many reasons. Students beginning to understand grammar do not need to be confronted with meter, variant forms, or other peculiarities that are often found in the poets. Rather, all but one selection are from prose.

Although limited primarily to prose, the readings include the genres of biography, oratory, philosophy, history, and scripture, over a course of 800 years (from the fifth century BCE to the third century CE). The reader is not meant to complement a comprehensive course in Greek grammar; however, it does establish a foundation for such a course in covering a broad range of topics and time periods. All readings have been chosen with care as well as with an eye to retaining the words of the author as much as possible. Alterations have been kept to a minimum.

Although an effort has been made to limit adaptations, some have certainly been made. Although the overriding goal in this reader was to preserve the "real Greek," there were cases where a particular word or phrase presented unnecessary difficulties for the beginning student. In these cases the challenging word was glossed and the text left uncorrupted. The three unedited texts (Lessons 24, 31 and 40) are signaled with an asterisk before the author or title. There is no textual critical work in this reader. The Greek text follows closely the Perseus Digital Library (http://www.perseus.tufts.edu) with the exception of the *Septuagint,* which is not in the Perseus Digital Library. For the *Septuagint,* the text follows closely the printed Rahlfs edition (Stuttgart: Biblia-Druck, 1935, 1979).

With respect to glosses, meanings given have been limited to those called for by the passages. In Lesson 24, the verb ἐμβάλλω has been glossed as "to feed" rather than the more common definition 'to throw in, or put in," because the syntax demands the former translation: "He ordered (his) friends to feed this forage to the horses . . . " Principal parts have been keyed to those covered by the grammar, so that the fourth principal part is not glossed until the reading for Lesson 31, and the remaining principal parts are given at Lesson 36 when Chase and Phillips does a complete summary of verbs. If a verb is regular, or a compound of a regular verb, or a compound of a verb that has already been introduced by Chase and Phillips, only the first principal part has been glossed (e.g., Lesson 25 περιπαθέω). Further, the English translation of the Greek verb is given in the infinitive. Nouns are given as gender/number/case in an abbreviated form, so masculine nominative singular would appear as m/nom/sing. Abbreviations are similarly given for tense, mood, and voice of verbal forms. Idioms have been glossed, and words not in the grammar but appearing in more than one reading have been glossed in each reading so each reading may stand alone.

In this reader, when a Greek term appears that is covered in the vocabulary of a later lesson in Chase and Phillips, that lesson is so indicated in the left column alongside the Greek term. At times a vocabulary term that was mentioned only in a note in an earlier lesson is glossed in a later lesson. For example, in Lesson 40 the reader comes across the Greek term, πειράω, which was not in any prior vocabulary list, but was mentioned in note five of Lesson 15 in Chase and Phillips. The term is glossed in the reading of Lesson 40. A point of grammar that appears in the reading and is introduced in a later lesson will be noted in the right hand column next to the English as there are times when Chase and Phillips merely mentions a point of grammar in a note, rather than addressing it more fully in the lesson. For example, the reading for Lesson 27 has the articular infinitive. Chase and Phillips mentions the articular infinitive (but hardly covers it) in a note on the reading in Lesson 15. So in the reading for Lesson 27 the articular infinitive is noted with a reference to Lesson 15.

Thus, it is my hope that this reader will aid students of ancient Greek in their demanding task of translating and understanding the language, and that they will be rewarded early in their career by meeting Diogenes Laertius, Xenophon, Plato, Plutarch and the *Septuagint*.

The Authors

The following is meant to give the student a mere sketch of the authors, characters, and works found in this reader. Some biographical information is given such as the authors' birth and death dates, or the time in which they flourished if the former is not known. Following this brief précis is a description of the work that has been chosen. For example, only selected dialogues of Plato have been used—namely the *Apology*, the *Phaedo*, and the *Republic*. Therefore, only these dialogues are discussed in the introductory section on Plato.

Xenophon

Xenophon the Athenian, son of Gryllus, was born about 430 BCE.[8] His early life was contemporaneous with the Peloponnesian War, and he knew Socrates. At the invitation of Xenophon's friend Proxenus, one of the Greek generals in the Persian Prince Cyrus' service, he joined in the campaign of Cyrus, who was attempting to depose his brother and gain the throne.

The *Anabasis* is Xenophon's recollection of these events. During the campaign, Cyrus was killed and Xenophon became one of the leaders of the ten thousand Greek mercenaries left in the heart of Persia. He describes a vivid tale of heroism, valor, courage, and sacrifice in the arduous journey home.

---

8. The date is disputed; other scholars argue for a date of 418 BCE.

Plato

Aristocles, nicknamed Plato on account of his broad shoulders (*platos*)[9], lived from 427/8 to 347/8 BCE.[10] His family was well established in Athens and had political connections. At the age of twenty, he met Socrates after whose death in 399 he travelled abroad. When he returned to Athens he began to teach philosophy.[11] The school, actually a garden and gymnasium, was named the Academy because it was situated next to the sacred precinct of the hero Academos.[12] Thus, Plato was about forty years old when he formally founded the Academy, and he taught there until his death. The Academy then had an uninterrupted life of 900 years, longer than any other institution of education in the West.[13]

Plato's writings have been "praised as the substance of Western thought."[14] It is with this respect that they have been included in this reader. The selections contained herein are certainly not meant to provide a comprehensive or even fairly representative selection of Plato's dialogues. Rather, these have been chosen for their wit, style, and substance.

The *Apology* is Plato's account of Socrates' defense before the Athenian jurymen. Socrates had been charged with corrupting the minds of the young and of believing in deities of his own invention instead of the gods recognized by the state. As a defense, Socrates gives an account of his life, showing that he has been merely following the command of god, and it has been by following this command that he has angered so many people who have now sought to condemn him on the charges above.

---

9. Freeman and Lowe, *A Greek Reader for Schools*, 73.

10. Authors who disagree as to the dates of his birth and death include: Hamilton and Cairns, *The Collected Dialogues of Plato*, xiii; Harvey, *The Oxford Companion to Classical Literature*, 331; and Freeman and Lowe, *A Greek Reader for Schools*, 73.

11. Harvey, *The Oxford Companion to Classical Literature*, 331.

12. Freeman and Lowe, *A Greek Reader for Schools*, 73.

13. Hamilton and Cairns, *The Collected Dialogues of Plato*, xiii.

14. Ibid., xiii.

The *Phaedo* is named after a devoted pupil of Socrates who was with him when he died. In this dialogue Phaedo, the mouthpiece of Plato, relates to his friends the circumstances and events leading up to and including the last moments of Socrates' life, during which he discussed the nature of the soul and life after death.

The subject matter of the *Republic* is justice and the virtues in being just. Socrates broadens the discussion to include not only individuals but states, and what the best possible state might be. A standard for human life is laid down. The soul "must be raised to behold the universal light . . . There is truth beyond this shifting, changing world and men can seek and find it."[15] To demonstrate this, Plato uses the allegory of the cave. Instead of going above the realms of ordinary experience, Plato goes below and "inverts a fire and shadows cast from it on the walls of a cave to correspond to the sun and the 'real' objects of sense," thus making our 'real' world the symbol of Plato's ideal world[16] and our 'shadows' the symbol of his earthly realm.

The *Septuagint*

The term *Septuagint* is Latin for seventy. It refers to a Greek translation of the Hebrew (Old) Testament, commonly referred to as LXX, the Roman numeral for seventy. The *Septuagint* takes its name from a legend whereby seventy scholars secluded on an island at the request of Ptolemy Philadelphus (284-247 BCE) forged a translation of the Hebrew in seventy days. It is now taken to be the work of Egyptian Jews working independently of one another and throughout different time periods, including and up to the first century CE.[17] Interestingly, the numbering of the Psalms in the *Septuagint* is not the same as the Hebrew it is translating. For example, in this reader the student sees *Septuagint* Psalm 22, which one might recognize as Psalm 23.

15. Ibid., 576.
16. Shorey, *Plato: The Republic*, 118.
17. Harvey, *The Oxford Companion to Classical Literature*, 390.

Plutarch

Plutarch, like Diogenes, was a Greek biographer. He was born about 46 CE and died in 120. He was a member of the college of priests at Delphi. His extensive travels took him to Alexandria, parts of Italy and Greece, and Rome, where he lectured on ethics. It is surmised that his works derive from his lecture notes.[18] He wrote many volumes, including *The Parallel Lives* and *The Moralia*. In the former work he compares such characters as Julius Caesar with Alexander, and Cicero with Demosthenes. Twenty-one other sets of lives are brought together to form the entirety of the work, in which he discusses the moral character of his subjects,[19] giving attention to anecdotes which provide the reader with a window to the soul of the subject. It is believed that his composition is a reaction to the decadence of Rome and her disregard of the old gods and philosophies. The *Lives* offer examples of moral guidance to pilot one through the audacious and impudent culture of the day.[20]

Diogenes Laertius

Diogenes of Laerte in Cilicia is a character of antiquity about whom we know very little, not even his place or date of birth.[21] It is known however that he wrote *Lives and Opinions of Eminent Philosophers*, a ten book account of eighty-two Greek thinkers from Thales (ca. 624 BCE) to Epicurus (ca. 341-270 BCE)[22] Internal evidence from the work indicates that Diogenes lived roughly from 200 to 250 CE.[23] Yet, it is difficult to ascertain very much about Diogenes because so much of his material is a reproduction of what he received.[24] According to modern standards, his work was

18. Ibid., 336.

19. Ibid., 336.

20. Ibid., 336–37.

21. Hicks, *Diogenes Laertius*, ix.

22. Harvey, *The Oxford Companion to Classical Literature*, 146.

23. Ibid., 146.

24. Hicks, *Diogenes Laertius*, xvii.

as uncritical as the age in which he wrote.[25] Although during the period of Diogenes' flourishing there existed many other books written on the subject, his work alone survives.[26] His *Lives* tells us much more about the philosophers than their philosophies and it is for that reason that the *Lives* is classified as biography.

25. Ibid., xv.
26. Ibid., ix.

Lesson 5

GRAMMAR ASSUMED:

Regular Verbs: Infinitive in indirect discourse

Socrates, before he drinks the hemlock, discusses the nature of the soul with his friend Cebes.

ΣΩΚ ἆρα οὐ νομίζεις τὴν ψυχὴν ἀεὶ ζωὴν φέρειν;

ΚΕΒ πάνυ γε.

ΣΩΚ ἆρα οὐ ζωῇ ἐναντίον ἔστιν;

ΚΕΒ ἔστιν.

ΣΩΚ τί;

ΚΕΒ θάνατος.

ΣΩΚ ἆρα ἡ ψυχὴ ἔχει τὸ ἐναντίον ᾧ αὐτὴ φέρει;

ΚΕΒ οὔ.

ΣΩΚ τί οὖν; τί ὀνομάζομεν ὃ τὴν τοῦ ἀρτίου ἰδέαν οὐδέποτε ἔχει;

ΚΕΒ ἀνάρτιον.

ΣΩΚ τί οὐδέποτε ἔχει τὸ δίκαιον;

ΚΕΒ τὸ ἄδικον.

ΣΩΚ τί οὐδέποτε ἔχει τὸ μουσικόν;

ΚΕΒ ἄμουσον.

ΣΩΚ ὃ οὐδέποτε ἔχει θάνατον τί ὀνομάζομεν;

ΚΕΒ ἀθάνατον.

ΣΩΚ οὐκοῦν ψυχή οὐκ ἔχει θάνατον;

ΚΕΒ οὔ.

ΣΩΚ ἀθάνατον ἄρα ψυχή.

ΚΕΒ ἀθάνατον.

Plato, Phaedo, 105.d.6-e.7

1

VOCABULARY

ἆρα	interrogative particle – expects a negative answer, whereas ἆρα οὐ expects a positive answer
ζωή, -ῆς, ἡ	life
πάνυ γε	certainly
ἐναντίον	opposite
τί	"what?"
αὐτή	f/nom/sing: "it" (refers to ψυχή)
οὖν	now, so
ὀνομάζω	call
ἰδέα, -ας, ἡ	concept
ἄρτιος, -α, -ον	complete
οὐδέποτε	never
μουσικός, -ή, -όν	musical
ἄμουσός, -ον	unmusical
οὐκοῦν	therefore
ἄρα	therefore

Lesson 8

GRAMMAR ASSUMED:

The Imperfect. The First and Second Aorists. Indicative and Infinitive

Diogenes Laertius relates some of the circumstances surrounding the trial and execution of Socrates.

Ἀντισθένης δὲ καὶ Πλάτων ἐν Ἀπολογίᾳ τρεῖς αὐτοῦ κατηγορῆσαι ἔφασαν, Ἄνυτον καὶ Λύκωνα καὶ Μέλητον· τὸν μὲν Ἄνυτον ὑπὲρ τῶν δημιουργῶν καὶ τῶν πολιτικῶν· τὸν δὲ Λύκωνα ὑπὲρ τῶν ῥητόρων· καὶ τὸν Μέλητον ὑπὲρ τῶν ποιητῶν, οὓς ἅπαντας ὁ Σωκράτης διέσυρε.

ὁ Σωκράτης καταδικάσθεις ἔφη πέντε καὶ εἴκοσιν δραχμὰς ἀποτίσειν. Εὐβουλίδης γάρ ἑκατὸν ἔφη ὁμολογῆσαι· "ἕνεκα," ἔφη, "τῶν ἐμοὶ διαπεπραγμένων τιμῶμαι τὴν δίκην τῆς ἐν πρυτανείῳ σιτήσεως."

οἱ δὲ θάνατον αὐτοῦ κατέγνωσαν, καὶ αὐτὸν εἰς δεσμωτήριον ἤγαγον ὅπου πολλὰ καλὰ κἀγαθὰ ἔλεξε καὶ μετ᾽ οὐ πολλὰς ἡμέρας ἔπιε τὸ κώνειον, ἃ Πλάτων ἐν τῷ Φαίδωνι ἔγραψε.

ὁ μὲν οὖν κατέλιπε τὸ σῶμα· Ἀθηναῖοι δ᾽ εὐθὺς μετέγνωσαν, ὥστε κλεῖσαι καὶ παλαίστρας καὶ γυμνάσια. καὶ τοὺς μὲν ἐφυγάδευσαν, Μελήτου δὲ θάνατον κατέγνωσαν. Σωκράτην δὲ χαλκῇ εἰκόνι ἐτίμησαν, ἣν ἔθεσαν ἐν τῷ πομπείῳ.

Diogenes Laertius, Socrates, 39, 41-43.

VOCABULARY

Ἀντισθένης, -ους, ὁ	Antisthenes, ca. 445 – ca. 360 BCE, considered the founder of the Cynics. Also, one of the most devoted followers of Socrates
Πλάτων,-ωνος, ὁ	Plato (see introduction)
Ἀπολογία,-ας, ἡ	*The Apology*, a work of Plato (see introduction)
τρεῖς/τρία, τρίων, τρισί(ν), τρεῖς/τρία (Lesson 37, section 2)	Three
αὐτοῦ	m/gen/sing "of him"
κατηγορέω,-ήσω, κατηγορήσα (+ gen)	to bring a charge against (someone)
Ἄνυτος,-ου, ὁ	Anytos (ca. 5th – 4th BCE), a wealthy Athenian, war hero and democratic leader who brought charges against Socrates
Λύκων,-ωνος, ὁ	Lycon, one of the three who brought charges against Socrates
Μέλητος,-ου, ὁ	Meletos, titular accuser of Socrates, perhaps the tool of Anytus, since Meletos was rather young at the time
ὑπέρ (+ gen)	on behalf of
δημιουργός,-οῦ, ὁ	a skilled workman
πολιτικός,-οῦ, ὁ	civil administrator
ῥητήρ,-ῆρος, ὁ	a speaker, politician

VOCABULARY (continued)

ἄπαντας	m/acc/pl "all"
Σωκράτης,-ους, ὁ	Socrates (469-399 BCE) famous philosopher condemned to death by an Athenian jury
διασύρω, διασυρῶ, διέσυρα	to tear to pieces
κατεδικάσθεις	m/nom/sing Perf. Pass. Ptc. "having been condemned"
ἀποτίνω, ἀποτείσω, ἀπέτεισα	Doric contraction of Fut. Act. Inf: to pay in full
Εὐβουλίδης,-ους, ὁ	Eubulides of Miletus, a teacher at Athens. He wrote a work against Aristotle, and is said to have taught Demosthenes
πέντε καὶ εἴκοσιν	twenty-five
ὁμολογέω,-ήσω, ὡμολόγησα	to agree (to)
ἑκατόν	one hundred
ἕνεκα (+ gen) (Lesson 29)	on account of
διαπεπραγμένων	n/gen/pl Pfct. Pass. Ptc. "things accomplished" (with dative of agent)
ἐμοὶ (Lesson 16)	"by me" 1st pers./sing./dat. personal pronoun
τιμῶμαι (Lesson 15)	here: "I adjudicate": from τιμάω cf. below

VOCABULARY (continued)

σίτησις,-εως, ἡ	consumption
σίτησις ἐν πρυτανείῳ	public maintenance
καταγιγνώσκω,- γνώσομαι, κατέγνων	to condemn (one) [+ gen] to (something) [+ acc]
αὐτόν	m/acc/sing "him"
δεσμωτήριον,-ου, τό	prison
ὅπου (Lesson 27)	where
πολλά	n/acc/pl "many"
κἀγαθά	(καί + ἀγαθά)
πολλάς	f/acc/pl "many"
πίνω, πίομαι, ἔπιον	to drink
κώνειον,-ου, τό	hemlock
Φαίδων,-ωνος, ὁ	*The Phaedo*, a work of Plato (see introduction)
εὐθύς (Lesson 20)	immediately
μεταγιγνώσκω	to have a change of mind
κλείω, κλείσω, ἔκλεισα	to close
παλαίστρα,-ας, ἡ	palaestra, wrestling school
γυμνάσιον,-ου, τό	gymnasium
φυγαδεύω,-σω, ἐφυγάδευσα	to banish

VOCABULARY (continued)

τιμάω, τιμήσω, ἐτίμησα (α-contract verb; Lesson 15)	to honor
χαλκός,-ή,-όν	f/dat/sing "bronze"
εἰκών,-όνος, ἡ	statue
τίθημι, θήσω, ἔθησα (1st pers. pl. ἐθέσαμεν) (Lesson 14)	to place
πομπείον,-ου, τό	a storehouse in Athens for sacred items used in the Panathenaic Festival. The storehouse was located between the Sacred and Dipylon Gates through which passed the road that led to Plato's Academy and the sacred city of Eleusis

Lesson 9

GRAMMAR ASSUMED:

Comparison of Adjectives and Adverbs

Socrates is questioning his accuser Meletus, who charges that Socrates is corrupting the young.

ΣΩΚ   λέγε, ὠγαθέ, τίς αὐτοὺς ἀμείνους ποιεῖ;

ΜΕΛ   οἱ νόμοι.

ΣΩΚ   ἀλλ᾽ οὐ τοῦτο ἐρωτῶ, ὦ βέλτιστε, ἀλλὰ τίς ἄνθρωπος, ὅς τοὺς νόμους οἶδε;

ΜΕΛ   οὗτοι, ὦ Σώκρατες, οἱ δικασταί.

ΣΩΚ   πῶς λέγεις, ὦ Μέλητε; οἵδε τοὺς νέους παιδεύουσιν τε καὶ βελτίους ποιοῦσιν;

ΜΕΛ   μάλιστα.

ΣΩΚ   πότερον ἅπαντες, ἢ οἱ μὲν αὐτῶν, οἱ δ᾽ οὔ;

ΜΕΛ   ἅπαντες.

ΣΩΚ   εὖ γε νὴ τὴν Ἥραν λέγεις καὶ πολλὴν ἀφθονίαν τῶν ὠφελούντων. τί δὲ δή; οἱ δὲ ἀκροαταὶ βελτίους ποιοῦσιν ἢ οὔ;

ΜΕΛ   καὶ οὗτοι.

ΣΩΚ   τί δέ, οἱ βουλευταί;

ΜΕΛ   καὶ οἱ βουλευταί.

ΣΩΚ   ἀλλ᾽ ἄρα, ὦ Μέλητε, μὴ οἱ ἐν τῇ ἐκκλησίᾳ, οἱ ἐκκλησιασταί, διαφθείρουσι τοὺς νεωτέρους; ἢ κἀκεῖνοι βελτίους ποιοῦσιν ἅπαντες;

ΜΕΛ   κἀκεῖνοι.

ΣΩΚ   πάντες ἄρα, ὡς ἔοικεν, Ἀθηναῖοι καλοὺς κἀγαθοὺς ποιοῦσι πλὴν ἐμοῦ, ἐγὼ δὲ μόνος διαφθείρω. οὕτω λέγεις;

ΜΕΛ πάνυ σφόδρα ταῦτα λέγω.

ΣΩΚ πολλήν γέ μου κατέγιγνωσκεις δυστυχίαν.

Plato, Apology, 24.d.10-25.a.12

VOCABULARY

λέγε	2nd sing. Pres. Act. Impv. from λέγω, λέξω, ἔλεξα to say, speak
ὠγαθέ (ὦ + ἀγαθέ)	"my good man"
τίς (Lesson 11)	m-f/nom/sing of the interrogative pronoun "who"
αὐτοὺς (Lesson 10)	m/acc/pl "them" (young people)
ποιεῖ (ε-contract verb; Lesson 15)	3rd sing. Pres. Act. Ind. from ποιέω,- ήσω, ἐποίησα to make (someone something)
τοῦτο (Lesson 10)	n/acc/sing "this"
ἐρωτῶ (α-contract verb; Lesson 15)	1st sing. Pres. Act. Ind. from ἐρωτάω, -ήσω, ἠρώτησα to ask
οἶδε (Lesson 40)	knows (3rd sing.)
οὗτοι (Lesson 10)	m/nom/pl "these"
Σώκρατης,-ους, ὁ	Socrates (469-399 BCE), a famous philosopher condemned to death by an Athenian jury
πῶς λέγεις	"how are you speaking?" what do you mean?

9

VOCABULARY (continued)

Μέλητος,-ου, ὁ	Meletos, titular accuser of Socrates, perhaps the tool of Anytus, since Meletos was rather young at the time
μάλιστα (Lesson 25)	"yes indeed"
πότερον . . . ἤ	indicates alternatives: here supply "does this apply to . . . or . . ."
ἅπαντες (Lesson 22)	m/nom/pl "all" (cf. πάντες)
εὖ γε	"excellent!"
νὴ τὴν Ἥραν	particle of strong affirmation with the accusative of the divinity invoked, here "Hera"
πολλήν (Lesson 18)	f/acc/sing from πολύς "much, many"
ἀφθονία,-ας, ἡ	abundance
ὠφελούντων	m/gen/pl Pres. Act. Ptc. "benefactors"
τί δὲ δή	"but what then"
ἀκροατής,-οῦ, ὁ	listener
βουλευτής,-οῦ, ὁ	Council member (There were about 500 members)
ἀλλ᾽ ἄρα	"but surely"
μή	expects a negative answer
ἐκκλησία,-ας, ἡ (Lesson 8, n. 3)	assembly
ἐκκλησιατής,-ου, ὁ	assembly member

VOCABULARY (continued)

διαφθείρω,-φθερῶ, -φθέρσα	to corrupt
κἀκεῖνοι (καὶ + ἐκεῖνοι) (Lesson 10)	m/nom/pl "those"
ἄρα (Lesson 11)	therefore
ὡς ἔοικεν	"as it would seem"
κἀγαθοὺς	(καὶ + ἀγαθοὺς)
πλὴν (+ gen) (Lesson 13)	"except"
(ἐ)μοῦ (Appendix 2)	gen/sing-1st pers. personal pronoun
πάνυ (Lesson 40)	certainly
σφόδρα	very much so
ταῦτα (Lesson 10)	n/acc/pl "these things"
καταγιγνώσκω	to condemn (one) [+ gen] to (something) [+ acc] cf. reading Lesson 8 above
δυστυχία,-ας, ἡ	ill fortune

Lesson 16

GRAMMAR ASSUMED:

δηλόω. Future of Liquid Verbs. Personal Pronouns

Psalm 22 of the Septuagint (Psalm 23 in English Bibles)

Ψαλμὸς τῷ Δαυιδ

Κύριος ποιμαίνει με, καὶ οὐδέν με ὑστερήσει.

εἰς τόπον χλόης, ἐκεῖ με ἔμεινε,

ἐπὶ ὕδατος ἡσυχίας ἐξέθρεψέν με,

τὴν ψυχήν μου ἐπέστρεψεν.

ἤγαγε με ἐπὶ ὁδούς δικαιοσύνης

ἕνεκα τοῦ ὀνόματος αὐτοῦ.

εἰ γὰρ καὶ ἵστημι ἐν μέσῳ σκιᾶς θανάτου,

οὐ φοβέομαι κακά, ὅτι σὺ μετ᾽ ἐμοῦ εἶ·

ἡ ῥάβδος σου καὶ ἡ βακτηρία σου, αὐταί με παρακαλοῦσι.

ἔστησας ἐνώπιόν μου τράπεζαν ἐξ ἐναντίας τῶν πολεμίων με·

ἐλίπανας ἐν ἐλαίῳ τὴν κεφαλήν μου,

καὶ τὸ ποτήριόν μου κατακλύζει,

καὶ τὸ ἔλεός σου καταδιώξει με πάσας τὰς ἡμέρας τῆς βίου μου,

καὶ ἐγὼ οἰκήσω ἐν οἴκῳ κυρίου εἰς μακρότητα ἡμερῶν.

Septuagint, Psalm 22

VOCABULARY

Κύριος,-ου, ὁ	The Lord
ποιμαίνω, ποιμανῶ, ἐποίμανα	to shepherd
ὑστερέω,-ήσω, ὑστερήσα	to come after
τόπος,-ου, ὁ	place
χλόη,-ης, ἡ	foliage
ἐκεῖ	there
ἐκτρέφω (ἐκ + τρέφω cf. Lesson 12)	to bring up (from childhood), to rear up
ἐπιστρέφω, ἐπιστρέψω, ἐπέστρεψα	to visit
δικαιοσύνη,-ης, ἡ (Lesson 4 n.9)	justice, righteousness
ἕνεκα (+ gen) (Lesson 29)	on account of
ὄνομα,-ατος, τό (Lesson 22)	name
μέσος,-η,-ον (Lesson 19)	middle
σκία,-ᾶς, ἡ (Lesson 3 n.7; Lesson 11 n. 2)	shadow
φοβέομαι (deponent verb, Lesson 25)	1st sing. Pres. Act. Ind. "I fear"
ῥάβδος,-ου, ἡ	rod

13

VOCABULARY (continued)

βακτηρία,-ας, ἡ	staff
παρακαλέω (παρα + καλέω)	to call to one's side, to be at one's side
ἐνώπιον (+ gen)	before
τράπεζα,-ας, ἡ	table
ἐναντίος,-α,-ον (ἐξ ἐ.)	opposite (opposite, over against)
λιπαίνω, λιπανῶ, ἐλίπανα	to anoint
κεφαλή,-ῆς, ἡ (Lesson 19)	head
ἔλαιον,-ου, τό	(olive) oil
κατακλύζω	to overflow
ἔλεος,-ου, ὁ	mercy
καταδιώκω, καταδιώξω, κατεδίωξα (cf. Lesson 21)	to pursue
πάσας (Lesson 18)	f/acc/pl from πᾶς "all, every (sing.)"
μακρός,-ά,-όν (Lesson 31)	long

Lesson 19

GRAMMAR ASSUMED:

Present, Future, and Second Aorist Participles Active of Ω and contract verbs

Julius Caesar is captured by pirates and held for ransom

πειραταὶ δὲ τὸν Καῖσαρα ἔλαβον πλέοντα περὶ τὴν Φαρμακοῦσσαν νῆσον, ἤδη τότε στόλοις μεγάλοις καὶ σκάφεσιν ἀπλέτοις κατεχόντων τὴν θάλατταν.

πρῶτον μὲν οὖν ᾔτησαν αὐτὸν λύτρα εἴκοσι τάλαντα, κατεγέλασεν ὡς οὐκ εἰδότων ὃν ᾑρήκοιεν, αὐτὸς δὲ ὡμολόγησε πεντήκοντα δώσειν· ἔπειτα τῶν περὶ αὐτὸν ἄλλον εἰς ἄλλην διήπεμψε πόλιν ἐπὶ τὸν τῶν χρημάτων πορισμόν, ἐν ἀνθρώποις φονικωτάτοις Κίλιξι μεθ᾽ ἑνὸς φίλου καὶ ἀκολούθων μένων, οὕτω καταφρονητικῶς εἶχεν, ὥστε πολλάκις προσέταττεν αὐτοῖς σιωπᾶν.

ἡμέρας δὲ τριάκοντα καὶ ὀκτώ, ἐπὶ πολλῆς ἀδείας συνέπαιζε καὶ συνεγυμνάζετο, καὶ ποιήματα γράφων καὶ λόγους τινὰς ἀκροαταῖς ἐκείνοις ἐχρῆτο, καὶ τοὺς μὴ θαυμάζοντας ἄντικρυς ἀπαιδεύτους καὶ βαρβάρους ἀπεκάλει, καὶ σὺν γέλωτι πολλάκις ἠπείλησε κρεμᾶν αὐτούς· οἱ δὲ ἔχαιρον, ἀφελείᾳ τινὶ καὶ παιδιᾷ τὴν παρρησίαν ταύτην νέμοντες.

ὡς δὲ ἧκον ἐκ Μιλήτου τὰ λύτρα αὐτοῖς ἔδωκε καὶ εὐθὺς ἐκ τοῦ Μιλησίων λιμένος ἐπὶ τοὺς πειρατάς ἐπῆλθε, καὶ καταλαβὼν ἔτι πρὸς τῇ νήσῳ ναυλοχοῦντας ἐκράτησε τῶν πλείστων. ἦλθε δὲ πρὸς τὸν διέποντα τὴν Ἀσίαν, ὡς ἐκείνῳ προσῆκει ὄντι στρατηγῷ κολάσαι τοὺς ἑαλωκότας.

ἐκείνου δὲ καὶ τοῖς χρήμασιν ἐποφθαλμιῶντος (ἦν γὰρ οὐκ ὀλίγα) καὶ περὶ τῶν αἰχμαλώτων σκέψεσθαι φάσκοντος ἐπὶ σχολῆς, χαίρειν κελεύσας αὐτὸν ὁ Καῖσαρ

εἰς Πέργαμον ἦλθε, καὶ προαγαγὼν τοὺς πειρατὰς
ἅπαντας ἀνεσταύρωσεν, ὥσπερ αὐτοῖς δοκῶν παίζειν ἐν
τῇ νήσῳ προειρήκει πολλάκις.

Plutarch, Caesar, 1.4-2.4

VOCABULARY

πειρατής,-οῦ, ὁ	pirate
πλέω, πλεύσομαι, ἔπλευσα	to sail
Φαρμακοῦσα,-ας, ἡ	Pharmakoussa, the modern Pharmaka, a tiny island about 12 miles East of Leros off the Southwest coast of Turkey
νῆσος,-ου, ἡ (Lesson 23, n. 7)	island
ἤδη (Lesson 31)	already
στόλος,-ου, ὁ	fleet
σκάφος,-εος, τό	ship
ἄπλετος,-ον	immense
κατέχω (κατά + ἔχω)	to possess
πρῶτον	at first (adverb)
αἰτέω, αἰτήσω, ἤτησαν (Lesson 31)	to ask someone for something (takes two accusatives)
λύτρον,-ου, τό	a ransom

LESSON 19

VOCABULARY (continued)

εἴκοσι (Lesson 37, paragraph 1)	twenty
τάλαντον,-ου, τό	a talent, a Greek weight of approximately 57 pounds of silver. One talent equaled 6000 drachma or denarii
καταγελάω,-άσομαι, κατεγέλασα (+ gen)	to mock
εἰδότων	m/gen/pl Pres. Act. Ptc. of οἶδα (cf. Lesson 40 and Appendix 7)
ᾑρήκοιεν	"they had seized" 3rd pl. Perf. Act. Opt.
ὁμολογέω	to agree
πεντήκοντα	fifty
διαπέμπω (δία + πέμπω)	to send off in different directions
πορισμός,-οῦ, ὁ	procuring, a means of getting
φονικός,-ή,-όν	murderous
Κίλιξ,-ικος, ὁ	a Cilician, the SE coast of present day Turkey, in ancient times an area known as Cilician was a notorious base for pirates; both Pompey and Cicero led military operations against them in 67 BCE and 51-50 BCE respectively.
ἑνός (Lesson 37)	m/gen/sing of εἷς, μία, ἕν "one"
ἀκόλουθος,-ον	follower, attendant

17

VOCABULARY (continued)

καταφρονητικός,-ή,-όν	contemptuous
προστάττω, προστάξω, προσέταξα	to command (+ dat) [someone] to do (+ infinitive) [something]
σιωπάω	to be silent
τριάκοντα καὶ ὀκτώ	thirty-eight
ἄδεια,-ας, ἡ	freedom from fear
συμπαίζω, συμπαίξομαι, συνέπαιζον	to joke with another
συγγυμνάζετο	3rd sing. Impft. Mid. Ind. from συγγυμνάζω, -σω "to exercise (oneself) with another"
ποίημα,-ατος, τό	poem
ἀκροατής,-οῦ, ὁ	listener
ἐχρῆτο (+ dat)	3rd sing. Impft. Act. Ind. from χράομαι, χρήσομαι, ἐχρησάμην "to employ"
θαυμάζω, θαυμάσομαι, ἐθαύμασα (Lesson 22)	to marvel at, to marvel, to admire
ἄντικρυς (adverb)	openly, outright
ἀπαίδευτος,-ον	uneducated
γέλως, γέλωτος, ὁ	laughter
ἀπειλέω,-ήσω, ἠπείλησα	to threaten, to promise

VOCABULARY (continued)

κρεμάννυμι, κρεμῶ, ἐκρέμασα	to hang
χαίρω, χαιρήσω, ἐχάρησα	to be delighted
ἀφέλεια,-ας, ἡ	simple-mindedness
παιδιά,-ᾶς, ἡ	play
παρρησία,-ας, ἡ	freedom of speech
νέμω, νεμῶ, ἔνειμα	to consider
ἥκω, ἥξω (Lesson 29)	to come
Μίλητος,-ου, ἡ	Miletus, an important Ionian city on the West coast of what is now Turkey
εὐθύς (Lesson 20)	at once, immediately
λιμήν,-ένος, ὁ	harbor
ἐπέρχομαι, ἐπελεύσομαι, ἐπήλθον (cf. Lesson 25)	to advance
καταλαμβάνω (κατα + λαμβάνω)	to overtake, seize
ναυλοχέω	to lie in harbor, ambush
κρατέω, κρατήσω, ἐκράτησα (+ gen) (Lesson 20)	to overcome, conquer
διέπω, διέψω	to manage (an affair)
προσήκω,-ήξω (+ dat)	to benefit one

VOCABULARY (continued)

κολάζω, κολάσω, ἐκόλασα	to punish
ἑαλωκότας	m/acc/pl Perf. Pass. Ptc. from ἁλίσκομαι, ἁλώσομαι, ἑάλων, ἑάλωκα "one having been taken" (a prisoner)
ἐποφθαλμιάω (+ dat)	to cast longing glances at
ἐκείνου... ἐποφθαλμιῶντος	"while . . . ." genitive absolute (see grammar Lesson 21, n. 6)
αἰχμάλωτος,-ον	prisoner
σκέπτομαι, σκέψομαι, ἐσκεψάμην	to consider, look at (a deponent verb)
φάσκω, —, —	to think, deem, expect, say
σχολή,-ῆς, ἡ	leisure, rest
κελεύσας	m/acc/sing 1st Aor. Act. Ptc. (Lesson 20)
Πέργαμον,-ου, τό	Pergamum, an important Hellenistic city in Mysia, in NW Turkey
προάγω, -άξω, -ήγαγον	to lead forward
ἀνασταυρόω,-ώσω, ἀνεσταύρωσα	to crucify
παίζω, παίξομαι, ἔπαισα	to play
προειρήκει (πρό + λέγω)	3rd sing. Perf. Act. Ind. "to say beforehand"

Lesson 24

GRAMMAR ASSUMED:

Past General Conditions and Indirect Discourse with ὅτι

Xenophon describes the generosity and character of Cyrus, a Persian contending for the throne.

Κῦρος γὰρ ἔπεμπε βίκους οἴνου ἡμιδεεῖς πολλάκις ὁπότε πάνυ ἡδὺν λάβοι, λέγων ὅτι οὔπω δὴ πολλοῦ χρόνου τούτου ἡδίονι οἴνῳ ἐπιτύχοι· τοῦτον οὖν σοὶ ἔπεμψε καὶ δεῖταί σου τήμερον τοῦτον ἐκπιεῖν σὺν οἷς μάλιστα φιλεῖς.

πολλάκις δὲ χῆνας ἡμιβρώτους ἔπεμπε καὶ ἄρτων ἡμίσεα καὶ ἄλλα τοιαῦτα, ἐπιλέγειν κελεύων τὸν φέροντα· τούτοις ἥσθη Κῦρος· βούλεται οὖν καὶ σὲ τούτων γεύσασθαι.

ὅπου δὲ χιλὸς σπάνιος πάνυ εἴη, αὐτὸς δὲ δύναιτο παρασκευάσασθαι διὰ τὸ ἔχειν πολλοὺς ὑπηρέτας καὶ διὰ τὴν ἐπιμέλειαν, διαπέμπων ἐκέλευε τοὺς φίλους τοῖς τὰ ἑαυτῶν σώματα ἄγουσιν ἵπποις ἐμβάλλειν τοῦτον τὸν χιλόν, ὡς μὴ πεινῶντες τοὺς ἑαυτοῦ φίλους ἄγωσιν.

εἰ δὲ δή ποτε πορεύοιτο καὶ πλεῖστοι μέλλοιεν ὄψεσθαι, προσκαλῶν τοὺς φίλους ἐσπουδαιολογεῖτο, ὡς δηλοίη οὓς τιμᾷ. ὥστε ἐγὼ μέν γε, ἐξ ὧν ἀκούω, οὐδένα κρίνω ὑπὸ πλειόνων πεφιλῆσθαι οὔτε Ἑλλήνων οὔτε βαρβάρων.

*Xenophon. Anabasis. I.9.25-28

VOCABULARY

Κῦρος,-ου, ὁ	Cyrus (d. 401 BCE), son of Darius II of Persia
βῖκος,-ου, ὁ	jar
οἶνος,-ου, ὁ	wine
ἡμιδεής,-ές	half-empty
πάνυ	very
οὔπω	a stronger form of οὐ
ἐπιτυγχάνω (+ dat) (ἐπι + τυγχάνω)	to find
δεῖται (+ gen) (Lesson 25)	3rd sing. Pres. Act. Ind. from δέομαι, δεήσομαι, ἐδεήθην "to ask" (deponent verb)
τήμερον	today
ἐκπίνω, ἐκπίομαι, ἔκπιον	to drink
χήν, χηνός, ὁ, ἡ	goose
ἡμίβρωτος,-ον	half-eaten
ἄρτος,-ου, ὁ	bread
ἥμισυς,-εια,-υ	half
ἐπιλέγω (ἐπι + λέγω)	to say in addition
ἤσθη (+ dat)	3rd sing. Aor. Pass. Ind. from ἥδομαι, ἡσθήσομαι, ἥσθην "to enjoy (something)" (deponent verb)

VOCABULARY (continued)

βούλεται (Lesson 26)	3rd sing. Pres. Act. Ind. from βούλομαι, βουλήσομαι, ἐβουλήθην "to wish" (deponent verb)
γεύσασθαι (+ gen)	Aor. Mid. Inf. from γεύω, γεύσω, ἔγουσα "to taste"
ὅπου (Lesson 27)	where/wherever
χιλός,-οῦ, ὁ	forage
σπάνιος,-α,-ον	scarce
δύναιτο (Lesson 25)	3rd sing. Impft. Act. Ind. from δύναμαι, δυνήσομαι, ἐδυνησάμην "to be able" (deponent verb)
παρασκευάσασθαι	Aor. Mid. Inf. from παρασκευάζω, παρασκευάσω, παρεσκεύασα "to procure for oneself"
τό ἔχειν	(articular infinitive) Lesson 15 n. 1
ὑπηρέτης,-ου, ὁ	assistant
ἐπιμέλεια,-ας, ἡ	foresight
διαπέμπω (δία + πέμπω)	to distribute
ἑαυτῶν (Lesson 20 n. 9 and Lesson 21 n. 3)	gen/pl of ἑαυτοῦ,-ῆς,-οῦ (of himself/herself/itself)
ἵππος,-ου, ὁ (Lesson 26)	horse
ἐμβάλλω (ἐμ + βάλλω)	here "to feed"
πεινάω, -ήσω, ἐπείνησα	to be hungry

VOCABULARY (continued)

πορεύοιτο (Lesson 29)	3rd sing. Pres. Act. Opt. from πορεύομαι, πορεύσομαι, ἐπορεύθην here "to journey"
ὄψεσθαι (Lesson 24)	Fut. Mid. Inf. from ὁράω, ὄψομαι, εἶδον (2nd Principal Part not given in Lesson 24)
προσκαλέω	to summon
σπουδαιολογέομαι, -λόγησα, -λογήθην	to converse seriously
πεφιλεῖσθαι	Pfct. Pass. Inf. from φιλέω "to have been loved"

Lesson 25

GRAMMAR ASSUMED:

The Middle and Passive Voices. Present Indicative, Middle and Passive. Future Indicative Middle. Clauses Expressing Fear.

Alexander tames Bucephalas to the wonderment of his father and others

ἐπεὶ δὲ Φιλονίκου τοῦ Θεσσαλοῦ τὸν Βουκεφάλαν ἀγαγόντος ὤνιον τῷ Φιλίππῳ τρισκαίδεκα ταλάντων κατέβησαν εἰς τὸ πεδίον δοκιμάσοντες τὸν ἵππον, ἐδόκει τε χαλεπὸς εἶναι καὶ μάλιστα δεινός, οὔτε ἀναβάτην προσιέμενος οὔτε φωνὴν ὑπομένων τινὸς τῶν περὶ τὸν Φίλιππον, ἀλλ᾽ ἁπάντων κατεξανιστάμενος, χαλεπῶς δὲ φερόντος τοῦ Φιλίππου καὶ κελεύοντος ἀπάγειν ὡς πάντως ἄγριον καὶ ἀκόλαστον, παρὼν Ἀλέξανδρος εἶπεν· "οἷον ἵππον ἀπολλύουσι δι᾽ ἀπειρίαν καὶ μαλακίαν χρήσασθαι μὴ δυνάμενοι," τὸ μὲν οὖν πρῶτον ὁ Φίλιππος ἐσιώπησε· πολλάκις δὲ αὐτοῦ παραφθεγγομένου καὶ περιπαθοῦντος, "ἐπιτιμᾷς σύ," ἔφη, "πρεσβυτέροις ὥς τι πλέον αὐτὸς εἰδὼς ἢ μᾶλλον ἵππῳ χρῆσθαι δυνάμενος;" "τούτῳ γοῦν," ἔφη, "χρησαίμην ἂν ἑτέρου βέλτιον."

γενομένου δὲ γέλωτος, εὐθὺς προσδραμὼν τῷ ἵππῳ ἐπέστρεψε πρὸς τὸν ἥλιον, ἐννοήσας ὅτι τὴν σκιὰν προπίπτουσαν καὶ σαλευομένην ὁρῶν πρὸ αὐτοῦ διαταράττοιτο. μικρὰ δὲ αὐτῷ παρακαλπάσας καὶ καταψήσας, ὡς ἑώρα πληρούμενον θυμοῦ καὶ πνεύματος, ἀσφαλῶς περιέβη.

τῶν δὲ περὶ τὸν Φίλιππον φοβουμενῶν μὴ Ἀλέξανδρος πάθῃ τι κακόν, ἦν ἀγωνία καὶ σιγὴ τὸ πρῶτον ὡς δὲ ὑπέστρεψεν ἀσφαλῶς σοβαρός, οἱ μὲν ἄλλοι πάντες ἀνηλάλαξαν, ὁ δὲ πατὴρ καὶ δακρῦσαί τι λέγεται πρὸς

τὴν χαράν, καὶ καταβάντος αὐτοῦ τὴν κεφαλὴν φιλήσας,
"ὦ παῖ," φάναι, "ζήτει σεαυτῷ βασιλείαν ἴσην Μακεδονία
γάρ σε οὐ χωρεῖ."

Plutarch. Alexander. 6

VOCABULARY

Φιλονίκος,-ου, ὁ	Philonikos
Θεσσαλός,-οῦ, ὁ	a Thessalian, one from Thessaly, a district of Northern Greece
Βουκεφάλας,-α, ἡ	Bucephalas, the name of a breed of Thessalian horses that became the name of Alexander's horse
Φιλίππος,-ου, ὁ	Philip of Macedon, father of Alexander
ὤνιος,-α,-ον	for sale
τρισκαίδεκα (cf. Lesson 37)	(τρεῖς + καί + δέκα) thirteen
καταβαίνω,-βήσομαι, κατέβησα (cf. Lesson 38)	to go down
δοκιμάζω,-σω, ἐδοκίμασα	to test
ἵππος,-ου, ὁ (Lesson 26)	horse
ἀναβάτης,-ου, ὁ	rider
προσίημι (πρός + ἵημι)	to let (something) come near to one
ὑπομένω	to submit to

VOCABULARY (continued)

φωνή,-ῆς, ἡ (Lesson 11, n. 3; Lesson 28)	voice
κατεξανίσταμαι, —, κατεξανέστην (+ gen)	to rear
ἄγριος,-α,-ον	wild
ἀκόλαστας,-ον	untamable
ἀπολλύω, ἀπολέσω, ἀπώλεσα (cf. Lesson 31 for a -μι form of the verb)	to lose
ἀπειρία,-ας, ἡ	inexperience
μαλακία,-ας, ἡ	weakness
χράομαι, χρήσομαι, ἐχρησάμην (Lesson 32)	to manage
σιωπάω,-ήσομαι, ἐσιώπησα	to be silent
παραφθέγγομαι, -φθέγξομαι	to interrupt
περιπαθέω	to be in a state of violent emotion
ἐπιτιμάω,-ήσω (+ dat) (cf. Lesson 15)	to rebuke (someone)
πρεσβύτερος,-α,-ον (Lesson 14, n. 10)	older, elder
γοῦν	at least
γέλος, γέλωτος, ὁ	laughter

VOCABULARY (continued)

προστρέχω, -δραμοῦμαι,-έδραμον (cf. Lesson 34)	to run towards
ἐπιστρέπω,-στρέψω, ἐπέστρεψα	to turn towards
ἐννοέω,-ήσω, ἐννώσας or ἐννοήσας	to notice (here the 3rd principal part is the Aor. Ptc.)
σκία,-ας, ἡ (Lesson 3, n. 7; Lesson 11, n. 2)	shadow
προπίπτω,-πεσοῦμαι, προὔπεσον (cf. Lesson 18)	to fall in front of
σαλεύω, σαλευθήσομαι, ἐσάλευσα	here "to dance"
διαταράττω,-ξω	to throw into great confusion, to confound utterly
παρακαλπάζω	to run beside (a trotting horse)
καταψήχω,-ξω, κατέψησα	to caress, stroke
ἑώρα (Lesson 40)	3rd sing. Impft. Act. Ind. of ὁράω: to see
πληρόω,-ώσω,— (+ gen)	to be full of (something)
θυμός,-οῦ, ὁ	vigor
πνεῦμα,-ατος, τό	spirit

VOCABULARY (continued)

ἀσφαλῶς	safely
περιβαίνω (cf. Lesson 38)	to mount
πάσχω, πείσομαι, ἔπαθον (Lesson 31)	to suffer
ἀγωνία,-ας, ἡ	anguish
σιγή,-ῆς, ἡ (Lesson 7, n. 6)	silence
ὑποστρέφω,-ψω, ὑπέστρεψα	to return
σοβαρός,-ά,-όν	proud
ἀναλαλάζω,-ξω, ἀνηλάλαξα	to shout aloud
δακρύω,-ύσω, ἐδάκρυσα	to weep
χαρά,-ας, ἡ	joy
φιλέω, φιλήσω, ἐφίλησα	here "to kiss"
φάναι (Lesson 40)	Pres. Act. Inf. of φημί, φήσω, ἔφησα "to say"
ζήτει (Lesson 28)	2nd sing. Pres. Act. Impv. of ζητέω "to seek"
ἴσος,-η,-ον (Lesson 8, n. 1; Lesson 9, n. 7)	equal
χωρέω, χωρήσω, ἐχώρησα	to contain

Lesson 27

GRAMMAR ASSUMED:

Contrary to Fact Conditions

Socrates admonishes those who have just passed a decree for his execution

οὐ πολλοῦ γ᾽ ἕνεκα χρόνου, ὦ ἄνδρες Ἀθηναῖοι, ὄνομα ἕξετε καὶ αἰτίαν ὑπὸ τῶν βουλομένων τὴν πόλιν λοιδορεῖν ὡς Σωκράτη ἀπεκτείνατε, ἄνδρα σοφόν—φήσουσι γὰρ δὴ σοφὸν εἶναι, εἰ καὶ μή εἰμι, οἱ βουλόμενοι ὑμῖν ὀνειδίζειν—εἰ γοῦν περιεμείνατε ὀλίγον χρόνον, ἀπὸ τοῦ αὐτομάτου ἂν ὑμῖν τοῦτο ἐγένετο· ὁρᾶτε γὰρ δὴ τὴν ἡλικίαν ὅτι πόρρω ἤδη ἐστὶ τοῦ βίου, θανάτου δὲ ἐγγύς.

λέγω δὲ τοῦτο οὐ πρὸς πάντας ὑμᾶς, ἀλλὰ πρὸς τοὺς ἐμοῦ καταψηφισαμένους θάνατον. λέγω δὲ καὶ τόδε πρὸς τοὺς αὐτοὺς τούτους. ἴσως με οἴεσθε, ὦ ἄνδρες Ἀθηναῖοι, ἀπορίᾳ λόγων ἑαλωκέναι τοιούτων οἷς ἂν ὑμᾶς ἔπεισα, εἰ μη ᾔσχυνα ἅπαντα ποιεῖν καὶ λέγειν ὥστε ἀποφυγεῖν τὴν δίκην. πολλοῦ γε δεῖ. ἀλλ᾽ ἀπορίᾳ μὲν ἡλίσκομην, οὐ μέντοι λόγων, ἀλλὰ τόλμης καὶ ἀναισχυντίας καὶ τοῦ μὴ ἐθέλειν λέγειν πρὸς ὑμᾶς τοιαῦτα οἷ᾽ ἂν ὑμῖν μὲν ἥδιστα ἦν ἀκούειν.

Plato. Apology. 38.c.-d.

VOCABULARY

οὐ πολλοῦ γ᾽ ἕνεκα χρόνου	"for the sake of not very much time"
αἰτία,-ας, ἡ	reputation
λοιδορέω,-ήσω, ἐλοιδόρησα	to revile
φήσουσι (Lesson 40)	3rd pl. Fut. Act. Ind. from φημί, φήσω, ἔφησα "to say"
ὀνειδίζω, ὀνειδιῶ, ὠνείδισα (+ dat)	to reproach
γοῦν (γε + οὖν) (Lesson 15, n. 4)	at least
περιμένω, περιμενῶ, περιέμεινα (Lesson 26, n. 2)	to wait around for
αὐτόματος,-η,-ον	of its own accord
ἡλίκια,-ας, ἡ	age
πόρρω τοῦ βίου	far advanced in life
ἐγγύς (+ gen)	near
καταψηφίζομαι, -ψηφιοῦμαι,-ψηφίσαμην	to condemn (+ gen) [someone] to (+ acc) [something]
ἴσως	perhaps
ἀπορία,-ας, ἡ (+ gen)	lack of

VOCABULARY (continued)

ἑαλωκέναι	"to have been condemned" Perfect Infinitive (Defective Passive) from ἁλίσκομαι, ἁλώσομαι, ἡλίσκομην, ἑάλωκα
αἰσχύνω, αἰσχυνῶ, ἤσχυνα	to be ashamed
ἀποφεύγω, ἀποφεύξομαι, ἀπέφυγον (cf. Lesson 13)	to escape
πολλοῦ γε δεῖ	"far from the truth"
μέντοι	however
τόλμα,-ης, ἡ	audacity
ἀναισχυντία,-ας, ἡ	shamelessness
τοῦ ἐθέλειν	articular infinitive (Lesson 15, n. 1)

Lesson 31

GRAMMAR ASSUMED:

Perfect

Life of Plato with reference to Xenophon, Antisthenes, and Socrates

Ἀλλά τοι Μόλων ἀπεχθῶς ἔχων πρὸς αὐτόν, "οὐ τοῦτο," φησί, "θαυμαστὸν εἰ Διονύσιος ἐν Κορίνθῳ, ἀλλ᾽ εἰ Πλάτων ἐν Σικελίᾳ." ἔοικε δὲ καὶ Ξενοφῶν πρὸς αὐτὸν ἔχειν οὐκ εὐμενῶς. ὥσπερ γοῦν διαφιλονεικοῦντες τὰ ὅμοια γεγράφασι, Συμπόσιον, Σωκράτους ἀπολογίαν, τὰ ἠθικὰ ἀπομνημονεύματα—εἶθ᾽ ὁ μὲν Πολιτείαν, ὁ δὲ Κύρου παιδείαν. καὶ ἐν τοῖς Νόμοις ὁ Πλάτων πλάσμα φησὶν εἶναι τὴν παιδείαν αὐτοῦ· μὴ γὰρ εἶναι Κῦρον τοιοῦτον—ἀμφότεροί τε Σωκράτους μνημονεύοντες, ἀλλήλων οὐδαμοῦ, πλὴν Ξενοφῶν Πλάτωνος ἐν τρίτῳ Ἀπομνημονευμάτων.

λέγεται δ᾽ ὅτι καὶ Ἀντισθένης μέλλων ἀναγινώσκειν τι τῶν γεγραμμένων αὐτῷ παρεκάλεσεν αὐτὸν παρατυχεῖν. καὶ πυθομένου, τί μέλλει ἀναγινώσκειν, εἶπεν ὅτι περὶ τοῦ μὴ εἶναι ἀντιλέγειν· τοῦ δ᾽ εἰπόντος· "πῶς οὖν σὺ περὶ αὐτοῦ τούτου γράφεις;" καὶ διδάσκοντος ὅτι περιτρέπεται, ἔγραψε διάλογον κατὰ Πλάτωνος Σάθωνα ἐπιγράψας· ἐξ οὗ διετέλουν ἀλλοτρίως ἔχοντες πρὸς ἀλλήλους. φασὶ δὲ καὶ Σωκράτην ἀκούσαντα τὸν Λύσιν ἀναγινώσκοντος Πλάτωνος "Ἡράκλεις," εἰπεῖν, "ὡς πολλά μου καταψεύδεθ᾽ ὁ νεανίσκος." οὐκ ὀλίγα γὰρ ὧν οὐκ εἴρηκε Σωκράτης γέγραφεν ἀνήρ.

*Diogenes Laertius. Plato. 34-35

VOCABULARY

τοι (enclitic) (Lesson 17, n. 10; Lesson 24, n. 4)	"you know"
Μόλον,-ωνος, ὁ	Molon
ἀπεχθής,-ές	hostile (Adverb + ἔχω: to be disposed in a certain manner: cf. below)
πρὸς αὐτόν	here refers to Plato
φησί (Lesson 40)	3rd sing. Pres. Act. Ind. from φημί, φήσω, ἔφησα "to say"
Διονύσιος,-ου, ὁ	Dionysius (ca. 430 – 367 BCE) a tyrant of Syracuse, to whose court Plato made a visit in a vain attempt to create a philosopher-king
Κορίνθος,-ου, ὁ	Corinth, the city located at the gateway to the isthmus, which made the city key to communication
Σικελία,-ας, ἡ	Sicily, which came to be ruled by Syracuse at the time of Dionysius
ἔοικε	"it seems"
Ξενοφῶν,-ῶντος, ὁ	Xenophon (see introduction)
εὐμενής,-ές	well-disposed
γοῦν (γε + οὖν) (Lesson 15, n. 4)	Stronger form of γε "at any rate, anyway"
διαφιλονεικέω,-ήσω	to love conflict
Συμπόσιον,-ου, τό	*Symposium*

VOCABULARY (continued)

Σωκράτους ἀπολογίαν	*Apology of Socrates*
τὰ ἠθικὰ ἀπομνημόνευματα	*Memorabilia* (moral treatises)
εἶτα	then
Πολιτεία,-ας, ὁ	*Republic* (a work of Plato)
Κύρου παιδείαν	*Cyropaedia* (a work of Xenophon)
Νόμοι,-ῶν, οἱ	*Laws* (a work of Plato)
πλάσμα,-ατος, τό	counterfeit
ἀμφότερος,-α,-ον (Lesson 37)	sing. "each" pl. "both"
τρίτῳ	understand "βιβλίῳ" with the numeral
μνημονεύω,-σω	remember
οὐδαμοῦ	nowhere
ἀναγιγνώσκω (cf. Lesson 22)	to read out loud
παρακαλέω (cf. Lesson 16)	to call for; to summon (one) [+ dat] (to do) [+ inf]
παρατυγχάνω (Lesson 33; cf. Lesson 21)	to be near
"ὅτι περὶ τοῦ μὴ εἶναι ἀντιλέγειν"	"that it was concerning the non-being (impossibility) of contradiction"
περιτρέπω (cf. Lesson 28)	to overturn

VOCABULARY (continued)

ὅτι περιτρέπεται	"that (the argument) overturns itself"
Σάθωνα,-ας, ἡ	*Sathon* (a work of the fifth century BCE philosopher, Antisthenes)
ἐπιγράφω (cf. Lesson 5)	to write, entitle
διατελέω,-τελέσω, διετέλεσα, διατετέλεκα	to continue (to be)
ἀλλότριος,-α,-ον	belonging to another
ἀλλοτρίως ἔχειν	to be at odds with
φασί (Lesson 40)	3rd pl. Pres. Act. Ind. from φημί, φήσω, ἔφησα "to say"
Λύσις, Λύσιδος, ὁ	*Lysis* (work of Plato)
καταψεύδομαι, -ψεύσομαι, κατεψευσάμην,-ψεύσμαι	to speak falsely
νεανίσκος,-ου, ὁ	a youth
ὀλίγος,-η,-ον	few
εἴρηκα (cf. Lesson 9)	Perf. tense of λέγω

Lesson 34

GRAMMAR ASSUMED:

The Imperative of Ω and contract verbs

The beginning of Book VII of Plato's *Republic* in which he discusses the analogy of the cave.

μετὰ ταῦτα δή, εἶπον, ἀπείκασον τοιούτῳ πάθει τὴν ἡμετέραν φύσιν παιδείας τε πέρι καὶ ἀπαιδευσίας. ἰδὲ γὰρ ἀνθρώπους οἷον ἐν καταγείῳ οἰκήσει σπηλαιώδει, ἀναπεπταμένην πρὸς τὸ φῶς τὴν εἴσοδον ἐχούσῃ μακρὰν παρὰ πᾶν τὸ σπήλαιον, ἐν ταύτῃ ἐκ παίδων ὄντας ἐν δεσμοῖς καὶ τὰ σκέλη καὶ τοὺς αὐχένας, ὥστε μένειν τε αὐτοὺς εἴς τε τὸ πρόσθεν μόνον ὁρᾶν, δεομένους ὑπὸ τοῦ δεσμοῦ ἀδυνάτους περιάγειν τὰς κεφαλάς, ὅρα δὲ φῶς αὐτοῖς πυρὸς ἄνωθεν καὶ πόρρωθεν καόμενον ὄπισθεν αὐτῶν, μεταξὺ δὲ τοῦ πυρὸς καὶ τῶν δεσμωτῶν ἐπάνω ὁδόν, παρ᾽ ἣν ἰδὲ τειχίον παρῳκοδομημένον, ὥσπερ τοῖς θαυματοποιοῖς πρὸ τῶν ἀνθρώπων πρόκειται τὰ παραφράγματα, ὑπὲρ ὧν τὰ θαύματα δεικνύασιν.

ὁρῶ, ἔφη.

ὅρα τοίνυν παρὰ τοῦτο τὸ τειχίον φέροντας ἀνθρώπους σκεύη τε παντοδαπὰ ὑπερέχοντα τοῦ τειχίου καὶ ἀνδριάντας καὶ ἄλλα ζῷα λίθινά τε καὶ ξύλινα καὶ παντοῖα εἰργασμένα, οἷον εἰκὸς τοὺς μὲν φθεγγομένους, τοὺς δὲ σιγῶντας τῶν παραφερόντων.

ἄτοπον, ἔφη, λέγεις εἰκόνα καὶ δεσμώτας ἀτόπους.

ὁμοίους ἡμῖν, ἦν δ᾽ ἐγώ.

Plato. *Republic.* 514.a-515.a

VOCABULARY

ἀπεικάζω,-άσομαι, ἀπείκασα, ἀπείκασμαι	to compare
πάθος,-εος, τό	experience
ἡμέτερος,-α,-ον	our
ἰδέ	here "picture"
οἷον	n/sing/acc as an adverb describing a state of being
κατάγειος,-ον (κατά + γῆ)	underground
οἴκησις,-εως, ἡ	dwelling
σπηλαιώδης,-ες	cavern-like
ἀναπεπταμένος	m/nom/sing Perf. Pass. Ptc. from ἀναπετάννυμι,-πετάσω, ἀνεπέτασα "to open"
εἴσοδος,-ου, ἡ	entrance
παρά (+ acc)	here and below "along"
σπήλαιον,-ου, τό	cavern
ἐκ παίδων	from childhood
σκέλος,-εος, τό	leg
αὐχήν,-ενος, τό	neck
πρόσθεν	before
ἀδύνατος,-ον	incapable
περιάγω,-ξω	to turn around

VOCABULARY (continued)

ἄνωθεν	from above
πόρρωθεν	from afar
κάω (Attic for καίω)	to burn
μεταξύ (Adv. μετά, ξύν)	between
ἐπάνω	above
δεσμώτης,-ου, ὁ	prisoner
τειχίον,-ου, τό	wall
παροικοδομέω,-ήσω, παρῳκοδόμησα	to build beside
θαυματοποιός,-οῦ, ὁ	puppeteer
πρόκειμαι	to lie
παράφραγμα,-ατος, τό	a low screen
θαυματόν,-οῦ, τό	puppet
τοίνυν	moreover
σκεῦος,-εος, τό	equipment
παντοδαπός,-ή,-όν	of every kind
ὑπερέχω (+ gen)	to rise above
ἀνδρίας,-αντος, ὁ	[statue] of a man
λιθινός,-ή,-όν	of stone
ξύλινος,-η,-ον	of wood
παντοῖος,-α,-ον	of all kinds

VOCABULARY (continued)

ἐργάζομαι,-άσομαι, εἰργασάμην, εἴργασμαι	to work
οἷον εἰκος	"as one would expect" (idiom)
φθέγγομαι, φθέγξομαι, ἐφθεγξάμην, ἔφθεγμαι	to speak
σιγάω,-ήσω, ἐσίγησα, σεσίγηκα	to be silent
παραφέρω (cf. Lesson 5)	to bring forward
ἄτοπος,-η,-ον	strange
εἰκών,-όνος, ἡ	image

Lesson 37

GRAMMAR ASSUMED:

Numerals

The Creation Story According to the Author of Genesis

Ἐν ἀρχῇ ἐποίησεν ὁ Θεὸς τὸν οὐρανὸν καὶ τὴν γῆν. ἡ δὲ γῆ ἦν ἀόρατος καὶ ἀκατασκεύαστος, καὶ σκότος ἐπάνω τῆς ἀβύσσου, καὶ πνεῦμα Θεοῦ ἐπεφέρετο ἐπάνω τοῦ ὕδατος. καὶ εἶπεν ὁ Θεός· γενηθήτω φῶς· καὶ ἐγένετο φῶς. καὶ εἶδεν ὁ Θεὸς τὸ φῶς, ὅτι καλόν· καὶ διεχώρισεν ὁ Θεὸς ἀνὰ μέσον τοῦ φωτὸς καὶ ἀνὰ μέσον τοῦ σκότους. καὶ ἐκάλεσεν ὁ Θεὸς τὸ φῶς ἡμέραν καὶ τὸ σκότος ἐκάλεσε νύκτα. καὶ ἐγένετο ἑσπέρα καὶ ἐγένετο πρωΐ, ἡμέρα μία.

Καὶ εἶπεν ὁ Θεός· γενηθήτω στερέωμα ἐν μέσῳ τοῦ ὕδατος καὶ ἔστω διαχωρίζον ἀνὰ μέσον ὕδατος καὶ ὕδατος. καὶ ἐγένετο οὕτως. καὶ ἐκάλεσεν ὁ Θεὸς τὸ στερέωμα οὐρανόν. καὶ εἶδεν ὁ Θεός, ὅτι καλόν, καὶ ἐγένετο ἑσπέρα καὶ ἐγένετο πρωΐ, ἡμέρα δευτέρα.

Καὶ εἶπεν ὁ Θεός· συναχθήτω τὸ ὕδωρ τὸ ὑποκάτω τοῦ οὐρανοῦ εἰς συναγωγὴν μίαν, καὶ ὀφθήτω ἡ ξηρά. καὶ ἐγένετο οὕτως. καὶ ἐξήνεγκεν ἡ γῆ βοτάνην χόρτου σπεῖρον σπέρμα κατὰ γένος καὶ καθ᾽ ὁμοιότητα, καὶ ξύλον κάρπιμον ποιοῦν καρπόν, οὗ τὸ σπέρμα αὐτοῦ ἐν αὐτῷ κατὰ γένος ἐπὶ τῆς γῆς. καὶ εἶδεν ὁ Θεός, ὅτι καλόν. καὶ ἐγένετο ἑσπέρα καὶ ἐγένετο πρωΐ, ἡμέρα τρίτη.

Καὶ εἶπεν ὁ Θεός· γενηθήτωσαν φωστῆρες ἐν τῷ στερεώματι τοῦ οὐρανοῦ εἰς φαῦσιν ἐπὶ τῆς γῆς, τοῦ διαχωρίζειν ἀνὰ μέσον τῆς ἡμέρας καὶ ἀνὰ μέσον τῆς νυκτός· καὶ ἔστωσαν εἰς σημεῖα καὶ εἰς καιροὺς καὶ εἰς ἡμέρας καὶ εἰς ἐνιαυτούς· καὶ εἶδεν ὁ Θεός, ὅτι καλόν. καὶ ἐγένετο ἑσπέρα καὶ ἐγένετο πρωΐ, ἡμέρα τετάρτη.

Καὶ εἶπεν ὁ Θεός· ἐξαγαγέτω τὰ ὕδατα ἑρπετὰ ψυχῶν ζωσῶν καὶ πετεινὰ πετόμενα ἐπὶ τῆς γῆς κατὰ τὸ στερέωμα τοῦ οὐρανοῦ. καὶ ἐγένετο οὕτως. καὶ εἶδεν ὁ Θεός, ὅτι καλά. καὶ ἐγένετο ἑσπέρα καὶ ἐγένετο πρωΐ, ἡμέρα πέμπτη.

Καὶ εἶπεν ὁ Θεός· ἐξαγαγέτω ἡ γῆ ψυχὴν ζῶσαν κατὰ γένος, τετράποδα καὶ ἑρπετὰ καὶ θηρία τῆς γῆς κατὰ γένος. καὶ ἐγένετο οὕτως. καὶ εἶδεν ὁ Θεός, ὅτι καλά. καὶ εἶπεν ὁ Θεός· ποιήσωμεν ἄνθρωπον κατ᾽ εἰκόνα ἡμετέραν καὶ καθ᾽ ὁμοίωσιν, καὶ ἀρχέτωσαν τῶν ἰχθύων τῆς θαλάσσης καὶ τῶν πετεινῶν τοῦ οὐρανοῦ καὶ τῶν κτηνῶν καὶ πάσης τῆς γῆς καὶ πάντων τῶν ἑρπετῶν τῶν ἑρπόντων ἐπὶ γῆς γῆς. καὶ ἐποίησεν ὁ Θεὸς τὸν ἄνθρωπον, κατ᾽ εἰκόνα Θεοῦ ἐποίησεν αὐτόν, ἄρσεν καὶ θῆλυ ἐποίησεν αὐτούς. καὶ εὐλόγησεν αὐτοὺς ὁ Θεός, λέγων· αὐξάνεσθε καὶ πληθύνεσθε καὶ πληρώσατε τὴν γῆν καὶ κατακυριεύσατε αὐτῆς καὶ ἄρχετε τῶν ἰχθύων τῆς θαλάσσης καὶ τῶν πετεινῶν τοῦ οὐρανοῦ καὶ πάντων τῶν κτηνῶν καὶ πάσης τῆς γῆς καὶ πάντων τῶν ἑρπετῶν τῶν ἑρπόντων ἐπὶ τῆς γῆς. καὶ ἐγένετο ἑσπέρα καὶ ἐγένετο πρωΐ, ἡμέρα ἕκτη.

Καὶ συνετελέσθησαν ὁ οὐρανὸς καὶ ἡ γῆ καὶ πᾶς ὁ κόσμος αὐτῶν. καὶ συνετέλεσεν ὁ Θεὸς ἐν τῇ ἡμέρᾳ τῇ ἕκτῃ τὰ ἔργα αὐτοῦ, ἃ ἐποίησεν, καὶ κατέπαυσεν τῇ ἡμέρᾳ τῇ ἑβδόμῃ ἀπὸ πάντων τῶν ἔργων αὐτοῦ, ὧν ἐποίησεν. καὶ ηὐλόγησεν ὁ Θεὸς τὴν ἡμέραν τὴν ἑβδόμην καὶ ἡγίασεν αὐτήν· ὅτι ἐν αὐτῇ κατέπαυσεν ἀπὸ πάντων τῶν ἔργων αὐτοῦ, ὧν ἤρξατο ὁ Θεὸς ποιῆσαι. Αὕτη ἡ βίβλος γενέσεως οὐρανοῦ καὶ γῆς.

Septuagint. Genesis. 1:1-2:4a

VOCABULARY

ἀόρατος,-ον	unseen
ἀκατασκεύατος,-ον	unfashioned
σκότος,-ου, ὁ (Lesson 24, n. 4)	darkness
ἐπάνω (+ gen)	above
ἄβυσσος,-ου, ἡ	the abyss
πνεῦμα,-ατος, τό	spirit, wind
διαχωρίζω, διαχωρίω, διεχώρισα, —, διακεχώρισμαι, — (cf. Lesson 17 n. 1)	to separate
ἑσπέρα,-ας, ἡ	evening
πρωί (adverb)	morning
στερέωμα,-ατος, τό	firmament
σύν + ἄγω	to gather together
ὑπακάτω	below
ξηρά,-ᾶς, ἡ	dry land
βοτάνη,-ας, ἡ	pasturage
χόρτος,-ου, ὁ	fodder
σπείρω, σπειρῶ, ἔσπειρα, ἔσπαρκα, ἔσπαρμαι, ἐσπάρην	to sow
σπέρμα,-ατος, τό	seed

VOCABULARY (continued)

ξύλον,-ου, τό	wood
κάρπιμος,-ον	fruitful
κάρπος,-ου, ὁ (Lesson 5, n. 5)	fruit
φωστήρ,-ῆρος, ὁ	star
φαῦσις,-εως, ἡ	illumination
σημεῖον,-ου, τό	constellation
ἐνιαυτός,-οῦ, ὁ	year
ἑρπετόν,-οῦ, τό	creeping thing
πετεινόν,-οῦ, τό	bird
πέτομαι, πετήσομαι, ἐπτόμην and ἔπτην	to fly
τετράπους,-ποδος, τό	herd animal
εἰκών,-όνος, ἡ	image
ἡμέτερος,-α,-ον	our
ἰχθύς,-ύος, ὁ	fish
κτῆνος,-εος	flocks
ἕρπω, ἑρψῶ, εἵπυσα	to creep
ἄρσην,-εν	male
θῆλυς,-εια,-υ	female
εὐλογέω	to bless
αὐξάνω	to increase

VOCABULARY (continued)

πληθύνω	to multiply
πληρόω,-ώσω, ἐπληρωσάμην, πεπλήρωκα	to fill up
κατακυριεύω	to gain dominion over/to lord over
συντελέω	to complete
ἁγιάζω, ἁγιάσω, ἡγίασα, ἡγίακα	to make holy
καταπαύω,-σω, κατήπαυσα, καταπεπαύκα	to cease from, rest

Lesson 40

GRAMMAR ASSUMED:

Conjugation of φημί

Socrates begins to defend himself against the charge brought by Meletus

περὶ μὲν οὖν ὧν οἱ πρῶτοί μου κατήγοροι κατηγόρουν αὕτη ἔστω ἱκανὴ ἀπολογία πρὸς ὑμᾶς· πρὸς δὲ Μέλητον τὸν ἀγαθὸν καὶ φιλόπολιν, ὥς φησι, καὶ τοὺς ὑστέρους μετὰ ταῦτα πειράσομαι ἀπολογήσασθαι. αὖθις γὰρ δή, ὥσπερ ἑτέρων τούτων ὄντων κατηγόρων, λάβωμεν αὖ τὴν τούτων ἀντωμοσίαν. ἔχει δέ πως ὧδε· Σωκράτη φησὶν ἀδικεῖν τούς τε νέους διαφθείροντα καὶ θεοὺς οὓς ἡ πόλις νομίζει οὐ νομίζοντα, ἕτερα δὲ δαιμόνια καινά. τὸ μὲν δὴ ἔγκλημα τοιοῦτόν ἐστιν· τούτου δὲ τοῦ ἐγκλήματος ἓν ἕκαστον ἐξετάσωμεν.

φησὶ γὰρ δὴ τοὺς νέους ἀδικεῖν με διαφθείροντα. ἐγὼ δέ γε, ὦ ἄνδρες Ἀθηναῖοι, ἀδικεῖν φημι Μέλητον, ὅτι σπουδῇ χαριεντίζεται, ῥᾳδίως εἰς ἀγῶνα καθιστὰς ἀνθρώπους, περὶ πραγμάτων προσποιούμενος σπουδάζειν καὶ κήδεσθαι ὧν οὐδὲν τούτῳ πώποτε ἐμέλησεν· ὡς δὲ τοῦτο οὕτως ἔχει, πειράσομαι καὶ ὑμῖν ἐπιδεῖξαι.

*Plato. Apology. 24.b-c.

46

VOCABULARY

κατήγορος,-ου, ὁ	accuser
κατηγορέω	to accuse
ἵκανος,-η,-ον	sufficient
ἀπολογία,-ας, ἡ	defense
πειράω (Lesson 15, n. 5)	to try
ἀπολογέομαι,-ήσομαι, ἀπελογησάμην, ἀπολελόγημαι	to defend oneself
αὖθις (lengthened form of αὖ)	again
ἀντωμοσία,-ας, ἡ	affidavit
ὧδε (adverb)	thus
πως (enclitic)	somehow
καινός,-ή,-όν	new
ἔγκλημα,-ατος, τό	accusation, charge
σπουδῇ χαριεντίζεται	here "to jest in earnest"
καθίστημι (κάτα + ἵστημι)	to set
προσποιέω	to pretend

VOCABULARY (continued)

σπουδάζω,-άσομαι, ἐσπούδασα, ἐσπούδακα, ἐσπούδαμαι, ἐσπουδάθην	to be serious
κήδω, κηδήσω, κήδεσα, κέκηδα	to distress
πώποτε	ever yet
μέλω	to care for

Bibliography

Adams, Charles Darwin. *Lysias: Selected Speeches*. London: University of Oklahoma Press, 1976.

Balme, Maurice, and G. Lawall. *Athenaze*. Oxford: Oxford University Press, 1991.

Balme, Maurice, and James Morwood. *Oxford Latin Course*. Oxford: Oxford University Press, 1988.

Chase, Alston H. and Henry Phillips, Jr. *A New Introduction to Greek*. 3rd ed. Revised. and enlarged. Cambridge, Massachusetts/London, England: Harvard University Press, 1961.

Freeman, C.E. and W.D. Lowe, eds. *A Greek Reader for Schools*. Oxford: Clarendon, 1971.

Goodwin, William W. and John Williams White, eds. *The First Four Books of Xenophon's Anabasis*. Boston, USA: Ginn & Co., 1889.

Hamilton, Edith and Huntington Cairns, eds. *The Collected Dialogues of Plato*. Bollingen Series LXXI; Princeton: Princeton University Press, 1961.

Harvey, Paul, ed. *The Oxford Companion to Classical Literature*. Oxford: Clarendon, 1955.

Hicks, R.D. *Diogenes Laertius: Lives of Eminent Philosophers*. vol.1, in The Loeb Classical Library. New York, New York: G.P. Putnam's Sons, 1925.

Shorey, Paul. *Plato: The Republic*, vol.2 in The Loeb Classical Library. Cambridge, Massachusetts: Harvard University Press, 1963.

Ullman, B.L., et al. *Latin for Americans*. New York, New York: Macmillan, 1981.

Wheelock, Frederick M. *Wheelock's Latin Grammar*. 7th ed. New York, New York: Collins Reference, 2011.